This book belongs to:

_____

_____

A new Light

For Erika Greelish, my beloved writing teacher for five years and counting. Thank you for giving me the tools to create this story.

— R. E.

A New Light
Text copyright © 2020 by Rosalie Eleanor
Illustrations copyright © 2020 by Tatiana Sorudeikina

This edition copyright © 2021 by Publishing House Ranok Limited
All rights reserved.
This book or any portion thereof may not be reproduced or used in any manner whatsoever without the express written permission of the publisher except for the use of brief quotations in a book review.
Created in 2020 by the KENGURU team.
First published in 2020 by Publishing House Ranok Limited.
ISBN: 978-617-09-6985-9
Publishing House Ranok Limited
135-27 Kibalchicha street, Kharkiv, Ukraine, 61071
KENGURU is a division of Publishing House Ranok Limited
For more information, contact KENGURU,
21a Kosmichna street, Entrance 1, Floor 8,
Kharkiv, Ukraine, 61145
Email: info@ikenguru.com.ua
https://ikenguru.com.ua/
https://www.facebook.com/kenguru2018/
https://www.instagram.com/kenguru2018
Book design by Bohdan Herashchenko

Publishing House Ranok Limited

A new Light

Written by Rosalie Eleanor
Illustrated by Tatiana Șorudeikina

CHAPTER ONE

If you can imagine a world of darkness, a world where all color, shape, and beauty has been stripped away, leaving you with nothing but an overwhelming longing for what you have lost, then you know what it was like for me when exactly that happened: the day that I lost my sight.

It has been almost a year since it happened, but I remember it like it was yesterday. It was in the middle of summer. My dad was outside washing Carol's car with my older brother Nate.

Carol is our next-door neighbor, a kind and gentle woman. Her house is cozy and warm, and she tells the most amazing stories, true and imaginary. She was outside as well, supervising the car-washing, and my mom was in the kitchen making lunch. I was wandering over to the living room to grab a book to read, when suddenly my vision began to get slightly fuzzy. I had never had any eye problems before, so this startled me. When it did not go back to normal, but only got worse, I began to panic. "Mom, mom, MOM!" I shouted, with increasing volume. I couldn't think straight. I started blinking rapidly and rubbing my eyes. It only got worse. "MOM!"

"What is it? Ashley, what's wrong?" asked my mom, probably rushing into the room, though it was hard to tell with my extremely blurry vision.

"M-mom," I stuttered, "My-my eyes, everything's all blurry and-and I don't know what's going on…" I trailed off, stumbling toward my mom's fuzzy image and breathing heavily.

"Hey, hey, Ashley, it's going to be okay, everything is going to be fine," she said, though as I fell into her trembling arms, I knew she was scared. I looked up at what I could see of her loving face and it turned out to be the last thing I ever saw. My world of sight disappeared forever, and a blackness darker than any night overtook me. I scarcely remember the rest. Dad, Nate, and Carol came in; I was rushed to the hospital; they did test after test after test. It is difficult to remember things from the day I became blind. Up to this point, my memories were most often associated with images. With only hearing and touch to remember events by, they became harder to grasp. I recall that day in a blur. The five of us, our small, but tight family, sat in a foul-smelling waiting room, anxiously anticipating the results of the tests. I was wrapped in their gentle, comforting embrace, and I clutched them tightly, determined to keep close the people who I knew would always be there. "Will you talk to me?" I whispered. "If I can't see you, I want to hear you."

"Of course, Ashley. Of course we will," Mom spoke softly back, so they did. They told me stories that made me smile, and for that one moment, it seemed as if everything might be okay after all. I heard a creak and then a click as a door opened and closed, and a woman said, "Ashley, Dr. Jehovah will see you now." I slowly stood up with the rest of my family, and with four sets of hands carefully guiding me we walked into a considerably better smelling room and sat down. The doctor explained in a patient, professional voice, "I am sorry to say that the results of your tests have concluded that you have an eye disorder called non-arteritic ischemic optic neuropathy. It occurs when there is a blockage of blood

supply to your optic nerve, a crucial part of the eye. Your case is particularly odd because this condition generally happens to people fifty years or older. You having it at only thirteen is very strange indeed. I am very sad to say that there is currently no found cure for ischemic optic neuropathy." There was a long and dreadful silence. I was too shocked to say anything. Thoughts were buzzing in my head like a swarm of bees. This was what I had been dreading. No cure. Those words floated in my head, ripping to shreds every last wisp of hope I felt. I would never see again. Not another sunset, clouds streaked with color. I would never see another snow-topped mountain or see the sunlight glistening off curved edges of water. I once hoped to see the Eiffel Tower or the Statue of Liberty or some beautiful thousand-year-old building in a far-off country. But I knew that I wouldn't. I was blind and would be for the rest of my life. That realization hit me so hard that even though I was surrounded by my family, I felt as though I was truly alone in the void of darkness from which it seemed I could never come out.

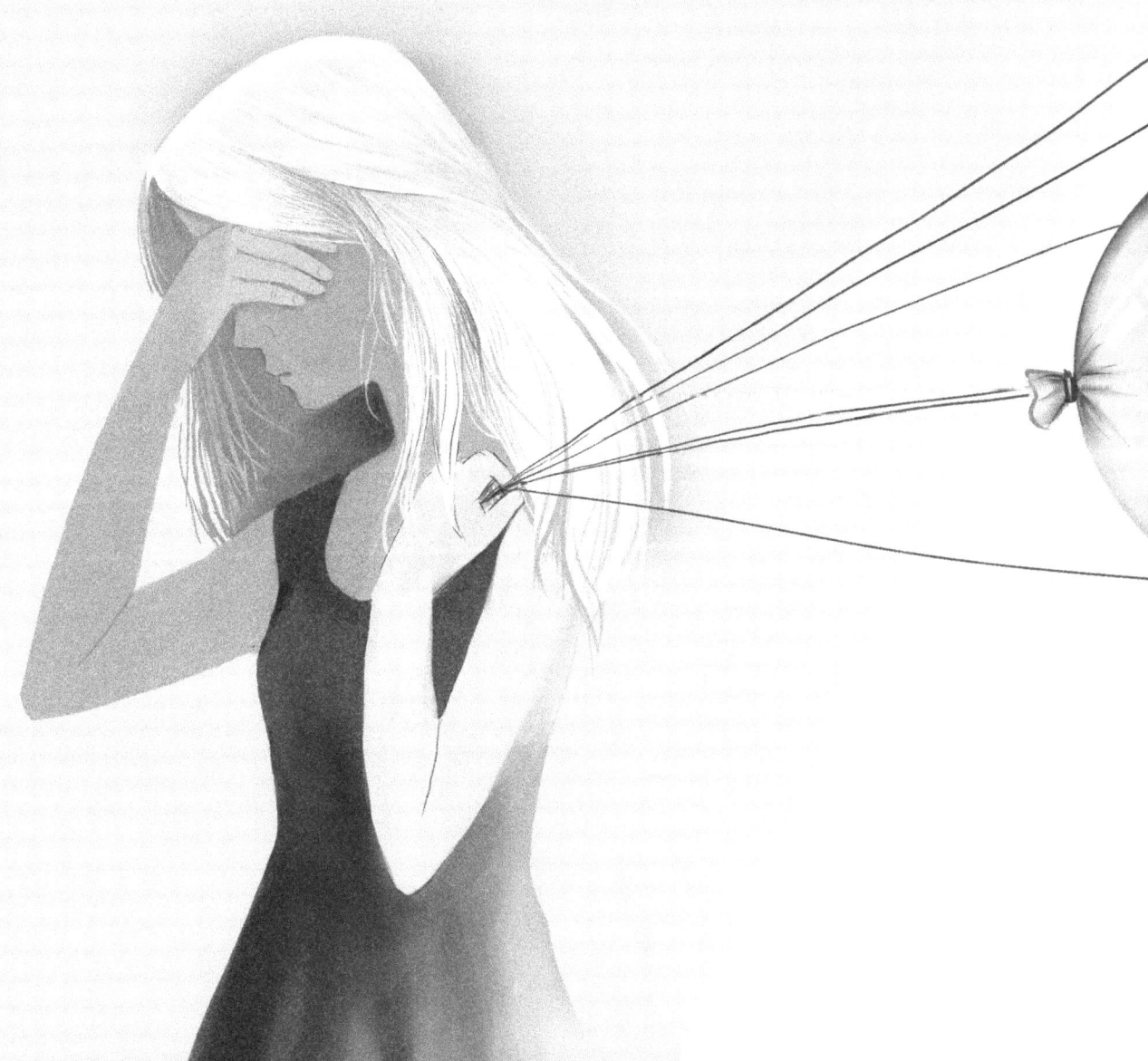

CHAPTER TWO

I hear the soft clink of Carol's knitting needles as I sit on her cozy, comfortable couch beside her. I feel her wrinkled skin; she seems so calm. I can't remember the last time she was tense, if she ever was.

"Carol," I ask, "how come you never get angry, or anxious? As long as I've known you you've never been anything but content."

The clinking stops. There is a small tap of wood against metal as she sets down her needles and I feel her arms wrap around me in a warm embrace. "Everyone gets angry sometimes, Ashley. Even if you don't see it," she says.

"I don't see at all," I reply.

She chuckles. "What I'm saying is not everyone puts their emotions on display. Some people express them openly, some ball them up inside and later cry in their rooms when they are alone because they prefer for people not to question them."

I consider this for a moment. "What do you do?"

"Why don't you tell me what you do first?" she asks in return.

I sigh. This is something she does often. I ask her a question and she makes me answer it before she does. Her answer is almost always better. "I think I express them more openly," I respond slowly. "I want people to know how I feel so they know how to respond to it.

That way there's no misunderstanding, and no one ever has to question how I feel. I think it is worse to suffer not knowing what someone is feeling than suffering from what you know they feel.

It is one of my least favorite things about being blind: not knowing. A lot of the time people express their emotions through facial expressions of nod of shake of the head. When I can't see that I don't know. I hate not knowing. How to respond, how to act, how to look, how to feel. That feeling of uncertainty, I can't stand it.

"I agree," Carol says.

I inwardly breathe a sigh of relief. "Now, what do you do?" I ask.

"I've done many things over the course of my life, but now I prefer to help others with their emotions, rather than overthink my own. I want to give people what I never had, although looking back, I wish I had: someone to listen."

"That doesn't count," I state.

She laughs again. "Well, it will have to, because that's all you're getting. Come on, it's almost dinner time, let's get you back home." And though I'm still not satisfied, I give in.

Up until a few months ago, I thought it would be all right after all. Even if I was blind, my family would always be there for me, to help me. Even if Dad was at work, or Nate was still in college up in Michigan, I would always have Mom. And at the end of the day, Dad would come home, and Nate would be here during summer and winter break. I would never be alone, or without any of the help I ever desired. And now, all I can think is, yeah right.

Mom is now seven months pregnant. And I once more feel all alone. The doctor recently told her to keep off her feet as much as possible. And as much as she's limited, I'm limited. Don't get me wrong, I'm really looking forward to having a younger sister, but I just feel like I can't do anything for her. I can't help her by just making her a meal because I can hardly make my own. I feel like I'm being needy, but I am blind. And she is pregnant, I remind myself as I sit on our couch with my mom. Maybe I am angry because I feel so useless, or maybe because I worry that mom might be upset with me when I can't help. I begin furiously fidgeting with my own fingers, turning these thoughts over and over in my mind. It is a weird habit, but ever since I became blind, I became obsessed with feeling things, trying to get pictures from the shapes and textures of things. As much as I can learn from that, I still miss color. Contrast, lights and darks, warms and cools, neutral and neon; they were so beautiful.

"Ashley, Ashley," my mom whispers excitedly, "come here, quick." I hurriedly slide over to the other end of the couch, next to Mom, discarding my thoughts. "Feel," she says, taking my hand and gently pushing it to her round belly. And then I feel it: a small yet determined kick. "Feel that?" I can tell from her voice she is happy. "That's your little sister, and she's kicking." I do feel it. My sister.

CHAPTER THREE

    I can't feel the ground below my feet. Or the wind, but I know they are there. I know they are there because I see the way the wind toys with the branches on the trees and the grass sways. I can't hear the water, but the rushing stream flows fast, crashing against rocks, spraying mist that won't touch my skin. The flowers blooming before my eyes are scentless but beautiful. The sun's golden rays cast no heat on me but illuminates my every surrounding. I am nether hot nor cold. Am I in the shade? But there are no shadows, only sun. Where...?
    My eyes shoot open, and I let out a large gasp. Darkness. It has happened again, I have had another dream. Tears begin rolling down my cheeks. Why do I have to dream? I miss sight enough without those terrible, tantalizing tastes of it to refuel my want. But I also want them, just to see. Even if it's just for a little. Then a dreadful realization dawns on me. I have been having dreams for a long time, but now is when I realize; compared to a year ago, the lines are getting fuzzier, the colors duller, and some things the shape isn't even right. My dreams are getting less vivid. I am forgetting how to see. I try to cling to every color, every shape, everything. I have to be able to at least think of pictures, of something. But as I attempt to grasp sight, it only fades more. I am alone in my bed. I don't know what time it is. Light or dark out, I'll probably never know. I lay back down, but my eyes won't close. They still yearn for something no one could ever give them. And though they know that, it can never satisfy their hunger.

There is no other way to put it, I am bored out of my mind. Being blind greatly decreases the things I can do on a sunny summer Saturday afternoon. When I could see, I loved doing quiet things by myself, like reading, writing, or reorganizing my room. Now, I can't read to myself, there's no imagining how bad my handwriting is, and what is the point in redoing my room if I can't even see it?

"Mom!" I yell.

"Yes?" she responds.

"Can I go to Carol's house?"

"I'll tell you what," interrupts my dad; I didn't even know he was there. "How about you and I go over to Freewind Park? We haven't been over there in a while."

I hesitate. Dad and I used to go to Freewind Park every Saturday. When I became blind, we stopped going. I haven't been to Freewind Park since.

"Okay," I reply slowly.

"Great," he says. "I'll be ready in five."

"Alright," I answer. I just hope I won't regret it.

My dad's firm but gentle hand is on my back, silently leading me into Freewind Park. The sun warms my skin as long blades of grass tickle my ankles. The rustle of branches accompanies the giggles of children as their footsteps bump on the metal of the playset. "It really has been a while," I whisper to myself. Dad takes my hand in his and squeezes it.

"And," he says, "it's been a while since we've had this."

I hear something come close to my face. I take a deep breath in through my nose. "Lasagna," I say, and smile. Whenever we used to come to the park, we would always have a picnic, which

usually consisted of one of my favorite foods, lasagna. My dad makes the best lasagna. He leads me to what I conclude from the upward slope to be the top of a hill. Then we sit on a blanket. It is probably the best lunch I've had in a year. The lasagna is warm and every bite I take is filled with stretchy, melted cheese.

"Do you still have room for dessert?" Dad asks after we finish.

"Did you?" I smile hopefully.

"Well, of course. We have to stick to tradition, don't we?" I lick my lips: Dad has brought Key lime pie. This was always our Saturday lunch, and Dad didn't miss a thing. The sharp tangy flavor combined with the creamy texture of the filling and the crunchy crust can't get any better than this. Why did I ever let being blind keep me from this?

"Dad," I question, "can we do this every Saturday, just like we used to?"

Dad wraps his arm around me, and I know the answer even before he says it. "I thought you'd never ask." It turns out it isn't even the lunch, or the majestic serenity of Freewind Park, but those words that make my day.

CHAPTER FOUR

    I sit with excited anticipation, squeezing Mom's hand. Nate is coming home today. When he got accepted into a college in Michigan, I knew he would love it there, but a small part of me wished he could stay. I fiddle with the pendent of my necklace, a smooth oval with the words carved into it: *We walk by faith and not by sight.* Not long after I became blind, my mom gave me this and I remember exactly what she said to me: "Ashley, you are a strong young woman and I know that whatever obstacles come

your way, you will always get back up again. I know you will always find a way to keep walking." I always hold those words with me in that necklace.

"Mom, when will he be home?" I inquire impatiently.

"I told you Ashley, he should be home any minute," Mom answers. Just at that moment the doorbell rings.

I jump up. "Is it him?" I yell. I hear my dad's quick, thumping footsteps moving toward the door. I hold my breath.

"Just the mailman," Dad says, sounding disappointed. I sigh and sit back down. The keys jingle and there is a small click as Dad unlocks the door. The door swings open. "Well hello, Mr. Mailman," says Dad in a friendly voice.

"Why, hello random man whom I have never met," responds a voice I wasn't expecting.

"Nate!" I cry as I run to the door. Dad and Nate both laugh at their joke.

"How are you, Nate?" I hear my dad ask.

"Great, I'm-" he is cut off by my tackle hug. He stumbles, regains balance, and wraps his bag-filled arms around me. "Ash, how have you been? I missed you so much!"

"I've been great! I felt the baby kick, and Dad and I went to Freewind Park!"

"That's amazing!" he exclaims. I can't believe he is finally home. I step aside to let everyone else say hello.

After talking with Nate for a few minutes my mom announces, "Dinner is ready, and I made chicken noodle soup."

"Mmm. Thanks, Mom," says Nate gratefully. Chicken noodle soup is Nate's favorite.

We sit around the table with our bowls in front of us. I smile. It has been a while since we were all together at our round table. Nate is on the right side of me, with my mom on the left, and Dad sits across from me. We all agree that when the baby comes, she will sit between me and Mom.

After dinner, I pull Nate aside. "Nate, come to my room," I whisper.

"Ok, I'm coming," he responds.

We walk into my room and proceed to ask what I have been wondering since he got here. "Well, what did they think?" I question excitedly.

"What did who think of what?"

"Oh, quit playing dumb. Your professors, of your poetry." Nate is an amazing poet, he just doesn't think he is. He only reads his work to me (mostly because I beg him to), but I know if he let other people read them, he could become famous. He just needs someone other then me to tell him how great they are. Now, he has to let his professors read them, and I am dying to know what they think.

"They actually really liked them," says Nate.

"I knew it!" I exclaim. "I told you, Nate, I told you they would love them!" I smile and hug him again.

"Thank you, Ash. If it weren't for you, I may have not even let them read them at all." I feel a bubbly feeling inside my stomach, like opening a soda bottle. A feeling fizzling up to the surface and running over. Joy.

"Ashley, come outside," Nate takes my hand. He's excited. About to show me something. I can feel it in his hand. He has that tingling anticipation. A fluttering hope. The way he is unsure about how much to squeeze my hand or whether to say more in fear of giving away his surprise. We sit beside an ancient oak tree, the rough bark up against my back.

"What is it?" I ask, "What do you want to show me?"

"How did you know I had something to show you? I swear, Ashley, you've acquired some kind of mind-reading ability since you became blind."

"No, I can just feel it. Now, what did you want to show me?"

"Just feel it? What are you some superhero, all of a sudden?"

"Nate!"

"Okay, okay. I have a poem to read you. If you want to hear it."

"I'd love too!" Nate has a poet's voice. It flows along with his writing, a graceful stream of words that warm my insides. He reads:

Something Sincere

There is something sincere today, with the whole earth alive,
For only with tears of the sky may the noble oak thrive.
One does not take, nor the other give,
But, in harmony the law in which nature must live.
The wind does not serve, and the hill does not bow,
This way always was and is now.
The sea will crash, and the clouds will bang,
But we will never forget moments the sun has sang.
Every leaf intertwined with fingers of breeze,
Every gust toying with branches of trees.
Ember of memory the fire will give,
In remembrance to care for all meant to live.
In that something sincere there is something to find,
Something to ease our hearts and our minds.
That we are part of this circle, this balance of life,
And this place is a blessing, to end all our strife.

CHAPTER FIVE

I am in the dining room, poking at the chicken and rice that lay before me. I twirl the chain of my necklace around my finger. The metal oval is cool and smooth. Suddenly, a metallic crash sounds and echoes through the room, making me whip my head up in shock.

"Mom, what was that?" I question, slightly panicked.

"It's okay, Ashley. The pots just fell out of the cabinet," my mother responds soothingly. I take a deep breath. It is easy to get startled by small sounds now. Who knows? Someone could be breaking into our house and I could think it was a lamp falling over! Maybe I am being too cautious, but better safe than sorry.

Shortly after I became blind, I was in our bathroom and noticed a siren wailing. The fire alarm. I was gripped by fear and dread. Quickly as I could, I stepped out of the bathroom. When the smell of smoke reached my nostrils, panic swelled in my chest and I dashed toward the door. An obstacle on the floor caused me to fall to the ground on my stomach, knocking my wind out. I had to get out. As soon as I regained my breath I sprang to my feet and out the door I flew.

"Ashley? Are you in here?" Mom said from inside the house. I was surprised at how calm she sounded.

"Mom, you have to get out of the house!" I shouted.

Then I heard her laughing. "It's okay, Ashley, the house isn't on fire."

"What?"

Her voice came closer, into the back yard where I was. "I just left something in the oven. It burnt, let out a lot of smoke, and set off the alarm."

"Oh," I said, embarrassed.

I hope nothing like ever happens again. What if something bad really does happen? What if I am in a situation I can't get out of? Or do something I think is right but is wrong, then it ends in disaster? It is like the world is trying to make me fear it, trying to make me afraid. Making me think that there is something hidden in the dark shadow of the unknown.

CHAPTER SIX

Drop. Drop. Drop. The rain pitter patters outside. I lay my hand on the cold glass on the window, longing to see this summer shower. Once, I would have loved to run about outside on a day like this. Bare feet in puddles, opening my mouth to the sky, enjoying a beautiful relief from sweat and sun. But what can I do now but sightlessly stare to somewhere beyond my present world? My eyes begin to mimic the way of the rain, filling with sorrowful tears. Then a wave of determination sweeps over me. *No. I will not let being blind keep me from what I want. I can do what I want, and I will. Sight or not.*

I take my hand off the window and march down the past the kitchen and dining room. I make my way down the hallway, turn left, and knock on Nate's door. "Come in," I hear from inside. I push open the door and close it behind me, then sit down beside Nate on his bed.

"I still don't know how you always know where I am. It's slightly scary, I'm not going to lie," Nate says.

"I'm not deaf," I respond. "on the contrary, I feel I have excelled in the sense," I finish matter-of-factly.

"Ahh, so you're an expert eavesdropper. I'll remember that," He says in a teasing tone.

"Well I didn't come in here to talk about my eavesdropping skills. Nate, I want to go on an adventure. It doesn't have to be anything crazy, I just want to do something I haven't done because I'm blind. Please?" I ask hopefully.

He thinks for a moment. "I guess we could. But we're not climbing mount Everest or anything," he warns.

"What are we going to do?" I eagerly inquire.

"That's my surprise. Be ready right after dinner tomorrow, okay?"

"Okay."

The jingling of keys sound from Nate's hand.

"Where are you going?" Mom asks.

"Ashley and I are going to get ice cream," Nate responds casually.

"Alright. Be back at eight o'clock at the latest."

We head out the door and seat ourselves in Nate's truck. Once we get going, Nate rolls down the windows and turns on the radio full blast. The wind whips my hair all around my face. I breath in the night air as it races past. A short while later, we stop.

"Where are we?" I ask.

"At the ice cream shop," he answers.

"We're actually going to get ice cream?"

"I'm not going to lie to mom. I said we were going to get ice cream, so we are. Although, I didn't say that was the only thing we were going to do." I smile. Nate leads me inside the ice cream shop and tells me the flavors. I choose pistachio and Nate butter pecan. Once we finish, we cross the road.

"Where are we now?" I ask in a tone of anticipation.

Nate takes my hand and leads me up to a thin metal thing, kind of like a balance beam. "You always said you wanted to walk on a railroad track. So here we are." A railroad track! The night is cool and crisp. Nate lets go of my hand and walks on the other side of the track. The crickets are chirping. There is a faint honk in the distance, and I hear cars zoom by to my left. I set one foot in front of the other, wondering how long the railroad has been here. Suddenly, I become conscious that the honking, now getting louder, is that of a train. Nate seems to realize at the same time.

"Ash, that's a train, we should get off the tracks." I hurry off, down the slope of rough rocks. "Ow!" I hear from behind me.

"Nate, are you okay?" The sound of the train gets louder.

"My ankle," he grunts. I run back and locate Nate. I try to help pull him off the tracks. We tumble down the rocks, reaching the bottom covered in scrapes. The train thunders past.

"I think I twisted my ankle," says Nate.

"I'm sorry," I say. I didn't mean for it to turn out like this.

CHAPTER SEVEN

"What happened?" Mom asks me when we arrive home.

"Well, after we got ice cream, we were walking on the railroad tracks for a little and Nate twisted his ankle," I respond. It was no use trying to lie to her.

Mom sighs. Dad quickly rushes off to take Nate to the hospital. *Great.* I think, *Now I have to deal with Mom all by myself.*

"I just didn't want being blind to keep me from doing things. I can still do things, I know I can. I just needed to prove it to myself," I explain, trying to excuse myself.

"You can't pretend that things haven't changed, Ashley, because they have. Your life isn't completely normal anymore and you can't do everything you used to. You have to accept that. You have your limits, as everyone does. You need to learn when you should say no, I expected more from you."

I begin to feel embarrassed. Is she really disappointed in me? It is my fault Nate got hurt. I should know better. My eyes filling with tears of guilt and regret, I run out the door of my house. In my yard I let my tears stream. I want to get away from it, from

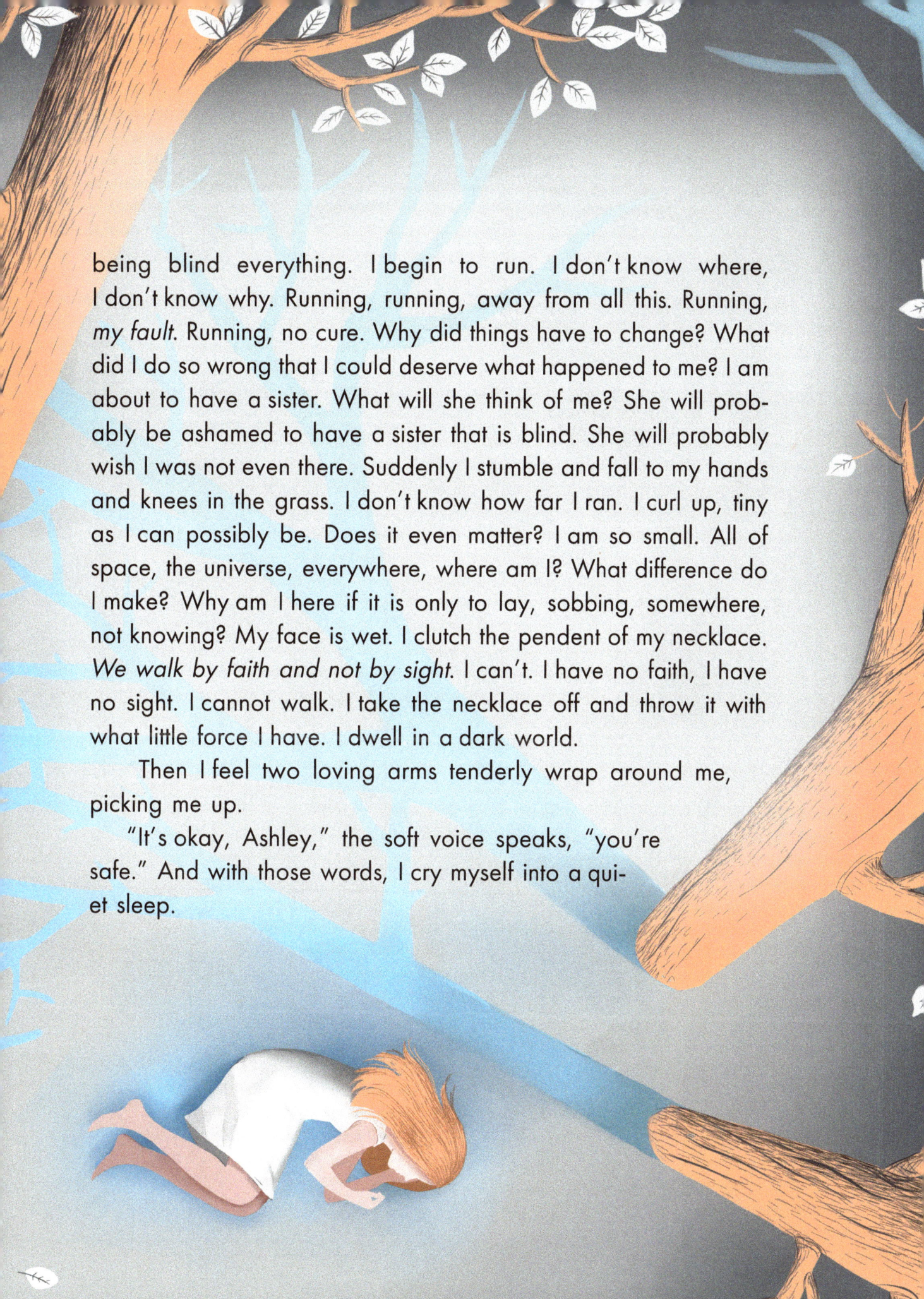

being blind everything. I begin to run. I don't know where, I don't know why. Running, running, away from all this. Running, *my fault*. Running, no cure. Why did things have to change? What did I do so wrong that I could deserve what happened to me? I am about to have a sister. What will she think of me? She will probably be ashamed to have a sister that is blind. She will probably wish I was not even there. Suddenly I stumble and fall to my hands and knees in the grass. I don't know how far I ran. I curl up, tiny as I can possibly be. Does it even matter? I am so small. All of space, the universe, everywhere, where am I? What difference do I make? Why am I here if it is only to lay, sobbing, somewhere, not knowing? My face is wet. I clutch the pendent of my necklace. *We walk by faith and not by sight*. I can't. I have no faith, I have no sight. I cannot walk. I take the necklace off and throw it with what little force I have. I dwell in a dark world.

Then I feel two loving arms tenderly wrap around me, picking me up.

"It's okay, Ashley," the soft voice speaks, "you're safe." And with those words, I cry myself into a quiet sleep.

CHAPTER EIGHT

I wake up in my own bed, nestled under the warm covers. I hear the creak of a rocking chair and the short metallic ringing of two knitting needles. Carol lays a comforting hand on my arm, then leaves the room. Two voices whisper in the hall. Footsteps enter, but they are not Carol's. I reach up to my chest. My necklace it still not there. I almost forgot that I threw it away. With that, the troubling thoughts of the past night return to me, but before I can think too much about it a voice interrupts.

"Hey, Ashley." My mother's voice is shaky; she has probably been crying. Her hand trembles as she grasps mine.

"Hey, Mom."

She takes a deep breath. "I just want to say I am really sorry. I was just worried that something worse could have happened than a twisted ankle, and I wasn't thinking about how you were feeling. You have experienced something many people, especially your age, have not had to go through. You have a right to whatever feelings you are having. I was really the one pretending, not you. You shouldn't have to feel alone."

Tears came to my eyes after my mom's honest words. "I thought that you were disappointed in me, in having a blind daughter. My sister probably will be."

"I am not disappointed in you, Ashley." I hear a tinge of guilt in her voice. "And I have no doubt that your sister is going to love you, just like we do," she continues reassuringly.

I smile.

"Oh, I almost forgot," she says. She puts something over my head.

I touch it. *We walk by faith and not by sight.* "My necklace," I say. "Thank you."

CHAPTER NINE

Nate shakes me awake in the middle of the night.

"Ashley, Ashley, wake up!" he demands urgently.

"What is it?" I ask, still half asleep.

"Mom's water broke! She's about to give birth to our sister and we have to get to the hospital."

I am suddenly wide awake. It's really happening! I hop out of bed and let Nate lead me into the car, not even bothering to change out of my pajamas.

When we enter the hospital, Mom and Dad are immediately ushered into one room, while Nate and I get stuffed into a waiting room. After the door closes, the room is quiet. All I can hear is my own heart, thumping with anticipation.

After what seems like an eternity, a nurse tells Nate and I that we can come in. The nurse opens the door for us. *My sister is in there*, I think with excitement. As we walk in, I hear the hushed voices of doctors and my parents. A smell unlike any other hits my nose. Nate is next to me, but I do not grab for his hand; I do not need his help to walk. I stop when I know there is a bed before me. I reach out my hand. Tiny, soft fingers wrap around my thumb and precious, "Ah," reaches my ears. The sound is the quietest in the room, but the joy it brings is louder than any voice. only a minute has passed, but already I love her with all my heart.

Her fingers are smaller than I could imagine, so small they seem unreal. But it is real, and so is the smooth, soft skin so new to this world touching my hand. Her hand is delicate, but strong. Someday this hand will do so much. This girl, who cannot even speak, will someday share words, ideas, and feelings with everyone around her. This child will never stop, she will achieve whatever she puts her mind to. She is but a baby now, but she will do so much, and she is my sister.

Mom puts a caring hand on my cheek, wiping away a tear.

"My sister," I whisper.

"Your sister," she responds quietly. "Her name is Faith."

I smile ear to ear, and with a voice filled with joy I say, "Welcome to the world, Faith."